This is a gift from the:

**Danville Library
Foundation**

The Lion
and the
Mouse

Retold by Diane Marwood

Illustrated by Anni Axworthy

Crabtree Publishing Company
www.crabtreebooks.com

Crabtree Publishing Company
www.crabtreebooks.com
1-800-387-7650

PMB 59051, 350 Fifth Ave.
59th Floor,
New York, NY 10118

616 Welland Ave.
St. Catharines, ON
L2M 5V6

Published by Crabtree Publishing in 2012
Printed in the U.S.A./052012/FA20120413

Series editor: Jackie Hamley
Editor: Kathy Middleton
Proofreader: Reagan Miller
Series advisor: Dr. Hilary Minns
Series designer: Peter Scoulding
Print and Production coordinator:
 Katherine Berti

Text © Franklin Watts 2009
Illustration © Anni Axworthy 2009

First published in 2009
by Franklin Watts
(A division of Hachette
Children's Books)

**Library and Archives Canada
Cataloguing in Publication**

Marwood, Diane
 The lion and the mouse / retold by Diane
Marwood ; illustrated by Anni Axworthy.

(Tadpoles: tales)
Issued also in electronic format.
ISBN 978-0-7787-7893-6 (bound).--
ISBN 978-0-7787-7905-6 (pbk.)

 1. Lions--Juvenile literature. 2. Mice--Juvenile
literature. I. Axworthy, Anni II. Title. III. Series:
Tadpoles (St. Catharines, Ont.). Tales

PZ8.2.M37Li 2012   j398.24'529757   C2012-902483-X

**Library of Congress
Cataloging-in-Publication Data**

CIP available at Library of Congress

This kind of story is called a fable. It was written by a Greek author called Aesop over 2,500 years ago. Fables are stories that can teach something. Can you figure out what the lesson in this fable is?

One day, tiny Mouse woke Lion up.

Lion was cross.
He caught Mouse
and was about
to eat him.

Mouse squeaked, "Don't eat me. I might be able to help you one day."

6

"How can a tiny mouse help me?" laughed Lion. But he let Mouse go.

Soon after, Lion got stuck in a hunter's net.

11

Days passed, and Lion got weaker. Then…

13

Mouse squeaked,
"Can I help you, Lion?"

"I'm stuck!"
cried Lion.

16

Mouse nibbled
and nibbled until
Lion was free.

"Thank you, Mouse!"
purred Lion.

Puzzle Time!

a

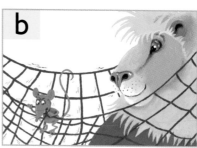

b

c

d

e

f

Put these pictures in the right order and tell the story!

tiny

fierce

huge

gentle

Which words describe Lion
and which describe Mouse?

Turn the page for the answers.

Notes for adults

TADPOLES: TALES are structured for emergent readers. The books may also be used for read-alouds or shared reading with young children.

The Lion and the Mouse is based on a classic fable by Aesop. Aesop's fables teach important principles about greed, patience, perseverance, and other character traits. Fables are a key type of literary text found in the Common Core State Standards.

IF YOU ARE READING THIS BOOK WITH A CHILD, HERE ARE A FEW SUGGESTIONS:

1. Make reading fun! Choose a time to read when you and the child are relaxed and have time to share the story.

2. Set a purpose for reading by explaining to the child that each of Aesop's fables teach a lesson. This information will help the reader understand the story and the features of the genre.

3. Encourage the child to reread the story and to retell it using his or her own words. Invite the child to use the illustrations as a guide.

4. Discuss the lesson of the story. Is the lesson important? Why or why not?

5. Give praise! Children learn best in a positive environment.

HERE ARE OTHER TITLES FROM TADPOLES: TALES FOR YOU TO ENJOY:

VISIT WWW.CRABTREEBOOKS.COM FOR OTHER CRABTREE BOOKS.

Answers

Here is the correct order!
1. d 2. c 3. f 4. a 5. b 6. e

Words to describe Mouse:
gentle, tiny

Words to describe Lion:
fierce, huge